Dear Parent:
Your child's love of reading starts here!

Every child learns to read in a different way and at his or her own speed. Some go back and forth between reading levels and read favorite books again and again. Others read through each level in order. You can help your young reader improve and become more confident by encouraging his or her own interests and abilities. From books your child reads with you to the first books he or she reads alone, there are I Can Read Books for every stage of reading:

SHARED READING
Basic language, word repetition, and whimsical illustrations, ideal for sharing with your emergent reader

BEGINNING READING
Short sentences, familiar words, and simple concepts for children eager to read on their own

READING WITH HELP
Engaging stories, longer sentences, and language play for developing readers

READING ALONE
Complex plots, challenging vocabulary, and high-interest topics for the independent reader

ADVANCED READING
Short paragraphs, chapters, an⸍ ⸍⸍⸍⸍⸍⸍⸍ ⸍⸍⸍⸍⸍⸍ for the perfect bridge to chap

I Can Read Books have introduced ⸍⸍⸍⸍⸍⸍ ⸍⸍⸍⸍ since 1957. Featuring award-winning au⸍⸍⸍⸍⸍ fabulous cast of beloved characters, I Can Read Books set the standard for beginning readers.

A lifetime of discovery begins with the magical words **"I Can Read!"**

Visit www.icanread.com for information
on enriching your child's reading experience.

A CHIPMUNK FAMILY CHRISTMAS

Library of Congress catalog card number: 2008932303
ISBN 978-0-06-171546-4
Book Design by Sean Boggs

❖

First Edition

I Can Read!

READING 2 WITH HELP

ALVIN AND THE CHIPMUNKS™

A CHIPMUNK FAMILY CHRISTMAS

Based upon the characters Alvin and the Chipmunks
created by Ross Bagdasarian
Story by Jon Vitti
Screenplay by Jon Vitti and Will McRobb & Chris Viscardi
Adapted by Susan Hill

HarperCollinsPublishers

One day near Christmas,
Alvin, Simon, and Theodore
left their tree and came to live
with a songwriter named Dave.

Dave was not happy.

"You can't live with me.
You're rodents!" said Dave.
"But we are the good kind
of rodents," said Alvin.

"We're cute," said Theodore.

"We can talk," said Simon.

"I noticed!" said Dave.

"That's creepy!"

Dave made the Chipmunks leave.

Then he heard singing.

He heard singing in

three-part harmony.

"You can sing?" Dave asked.

"But isn't that creepy, Dave?"

asked Alvin.

"No," said Dave, "That's amazing!"

Dave let the Chipmunks stay.

"Don't tell your friends

about this," Dave said.

"I don't want a bunch of rabbits

and skunks in here."

"You're our only friend,"

said Theodore.

Dave didn't want chipmunk friends.

"Let's just start with me being

your songwriter," he said.

Dave tucked the Chipmunks into bed.
Then he stayed up late and wrote
a Christmas song for them to sing.

The very next day,
Dave put the Chipmunks in a box
and took them to the record company.
But the Chipmunks
were too scared
to sing for anyone
but Dave.

"Great," said Dave.

"Christmas is coming,

and nobody will hear our song."

"Christmas!" shouted the Chipmunks.

"We've never had Christmas!"

"Christmas is for family,"

Dave said.

"Don't you have parents?"

Alvin shook his head.

"You're all we've got," he said.

Dave gave Simon a pair of glasses.
"This must be what Christmas
is like!" said Simon.

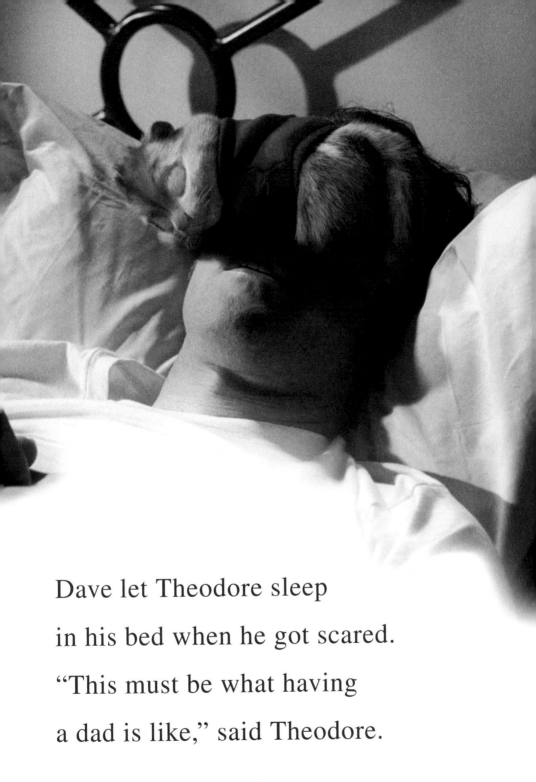

Dave let Theodore sleep
in his bed when he got scared.
"This must be what having
a dad is like," said Theodore.

19

Dave made tiny costumes
for the Chipmunks.
Alvin's even had an "A" on it.
"This must be what having
clothes is like," said Alvin.

The Chipmunks made Dave's house
very messy.

"This must be what having kids is like!" Dave said.

"Allllviiiinnn!" shouted Dave.

Dave got fired from his job.
The Chipmunks felt bad.
They snuck out of the house
and sang Dave's Christmas song
for the record company.

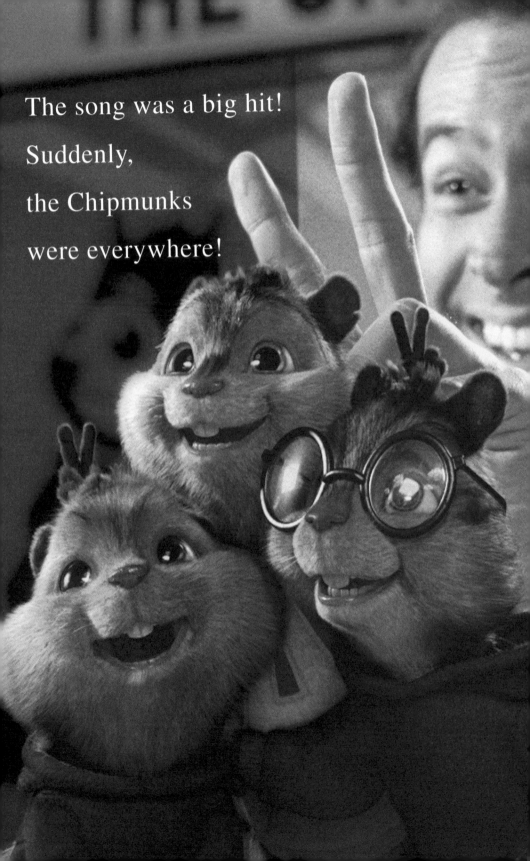

The song was a big hit!
Suddenly,
the Chipmunks
were everywhere!

Their pictures were in magazines,
their songs played on the radio,
and their concerts sold out!

But the best thing of all

was checking off the days

until Christmas on Dave's calendar.

Christmas finally came.

Simon gave Dave a compass.

Alvin gave Dave a wallet.

It was Dave's wallet.

Theodore made him a picture.

"Pineapples?" said Dave.

"Those aren't pineapples!"

said Theodore.

"That's our family!"

"We are not a regular family,"
said Alvin.

"We are not a pineapple family,"
said Theodore.

"We are not even a human family,"
said Simon.

"But, we are a family," Dave said.
Suddenly, Alvin and the Chipmunks
knew what Christmas was all about.
And Dave did, too.

"Merry Christmas, Dave,"
said Alvin.
"Merry Christmas," said Dave.